Good Morning, Sunshine

A GRANDPA STORY

Written and Illustrated by Sharon McKenna

red
cygnet™
PRESS

San Diego, California

red
cygnet™
PRESS

To my family, who always believed I could do this. – S.M.

Cover and book design: Amy Stirnkorb

First Edition 2007
10 9 8 7 6 5 4 3 2
Printed in China

Library of Congress Cataloging-in-Publication Data
is available at our website: www.redcygnet.com

I love to stay overnight at my grandpa's house.

But, sometimes in the
morning when I wake up
I am grumpy.

My grandpa takes me on
his lap and says,
"Katie come with me!"

We open the front door and we yell,
"Good morning sunshine!"
And I feel better.

I love to go for walks
with my grandpa.

But, sometimes in the
morning I don't want
to get dressed.

My grandpa holds my hand, and we walk

to the closet. We
open the door, look
inside and giggle,

"Good morning clothes!"
And I feel better.

I love to play outside
with my dolly,
Baby Katie.

But, sometimes in the
afternoon it's raining
and I can't go
out to play.

My grandpa throws me over
his shoulder, and we open
the front door.

We yell,
"Good
afternoon
raindrops!"

And I feel
better.

I love to eat dinner
with my grandpa.

But, sometimes
I don't want to eat
my vegetables.

My grandpa walks me over to the refrigerator.

We open the door,
and we say,
"Good evening broccoli!"
And I feel better.

I love to hear my bedtime stories
when I sleep at grandpa's.

But, sometimes I don't want
to go to bed.

My grandpa holds me close
and says, "Katie, come with me."

We open the front door and
we whisper..."

"Goodnight
Stars!"

And I feel
better.

I love to visit my grandpa.

He teaches me how
to feel better.